CW00420187

Nathaniel Hawthorne (July 4, 1804 – May 19, 1864) was an American novelist, dark romantic, and short story writer. His works often focus on history, morality, and religion. He was born in 1804 in Salem, Massachusetts, to Nathaniel Hathorne and the former Elizabeth Clarke Manning. His ancestors include John Hathorne, the only judge involved in the Salem witch trials who never repented of his actions. He entered Bowdoin College in 1821, was elected to Phi Beta Kappa in 1824, and graduated in 1825. He published his first work in 1828, the novel Fanshawe; he later tried to suppress it, feeling that it was not equal to the standard of his later work. He published several short stories in periodicals, which he collected in 1837 as Twice-Told Tales. The next year, he became engaged to Sophia Peabody. He worked at the Boston Custom House and joined Brook Farm, a transcendentalist community, before marrying Peabody in 1842. The couple moved to The Old Manse in Concord, Massachusetts, later moving to Salem, the Berkshires, then to The Wayside in Concord. (Source: Wikipedia)

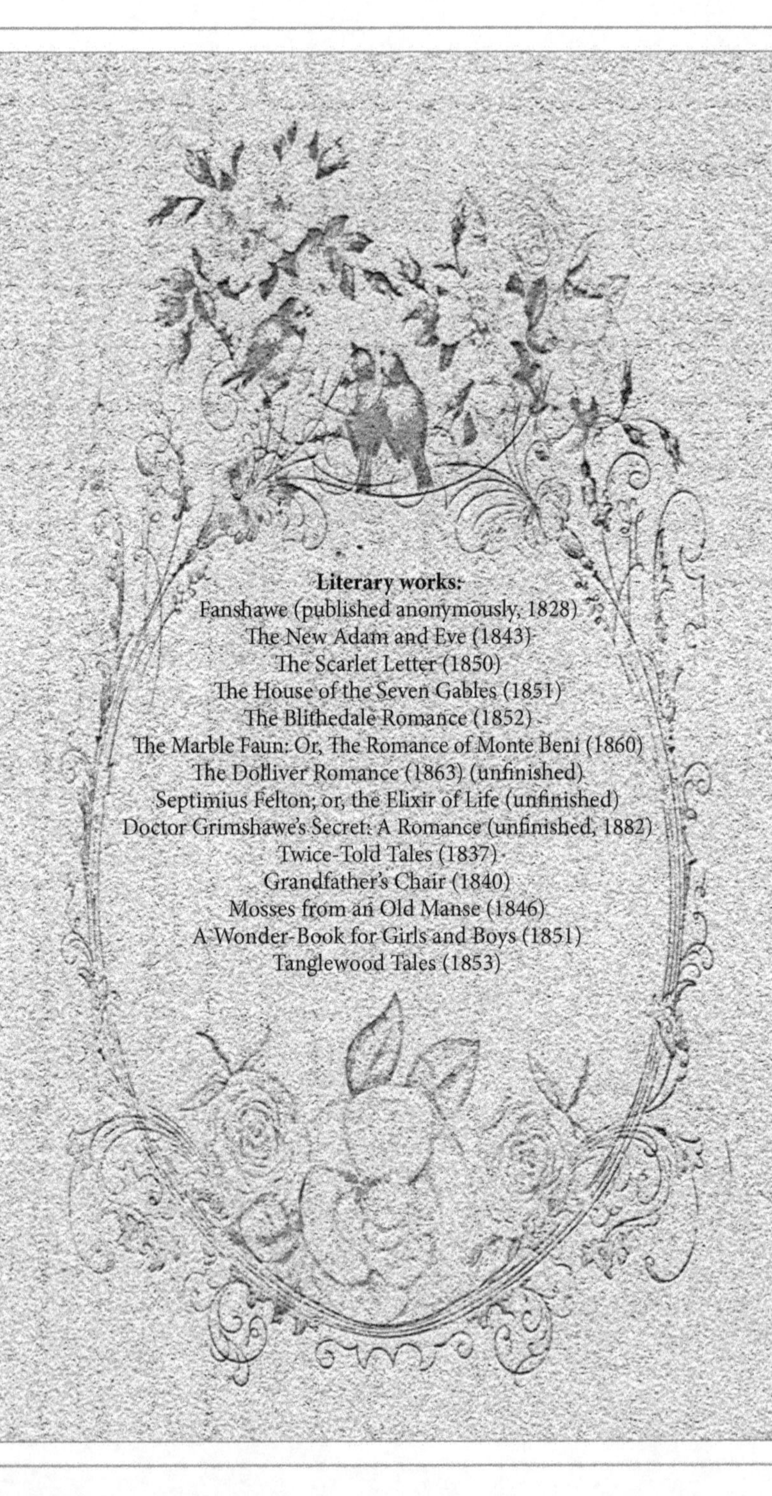

Literary works:

Fanshawe (published anonymously, 1828)
The New Adam and Eve (1843)
The Scarlet Letter (1850)
The House of the Seven Gables (1851)
The Blithedale Romance (1852)
The Marble Faun: Or, The Romance of Monte Beni (1860)
The Dolliver Romance (1863) (unfinished)
Septimius Felton; or, the Elixir of Life (unfinished)
Doctor Grimshawe's Secret: A Romance (unfinished, 1882)
Twice-Told Tales (1837)
Grandfather's Chair (1840)
Mosses from an Old Manse (1846)
A Wonder-Book for Girls and Boys (1851)
Tanglewood Tales (1853)

OTHER TALES
AND SKETCHES
NATHANIEL HAWTHORNE
PRINCE CLASSICS

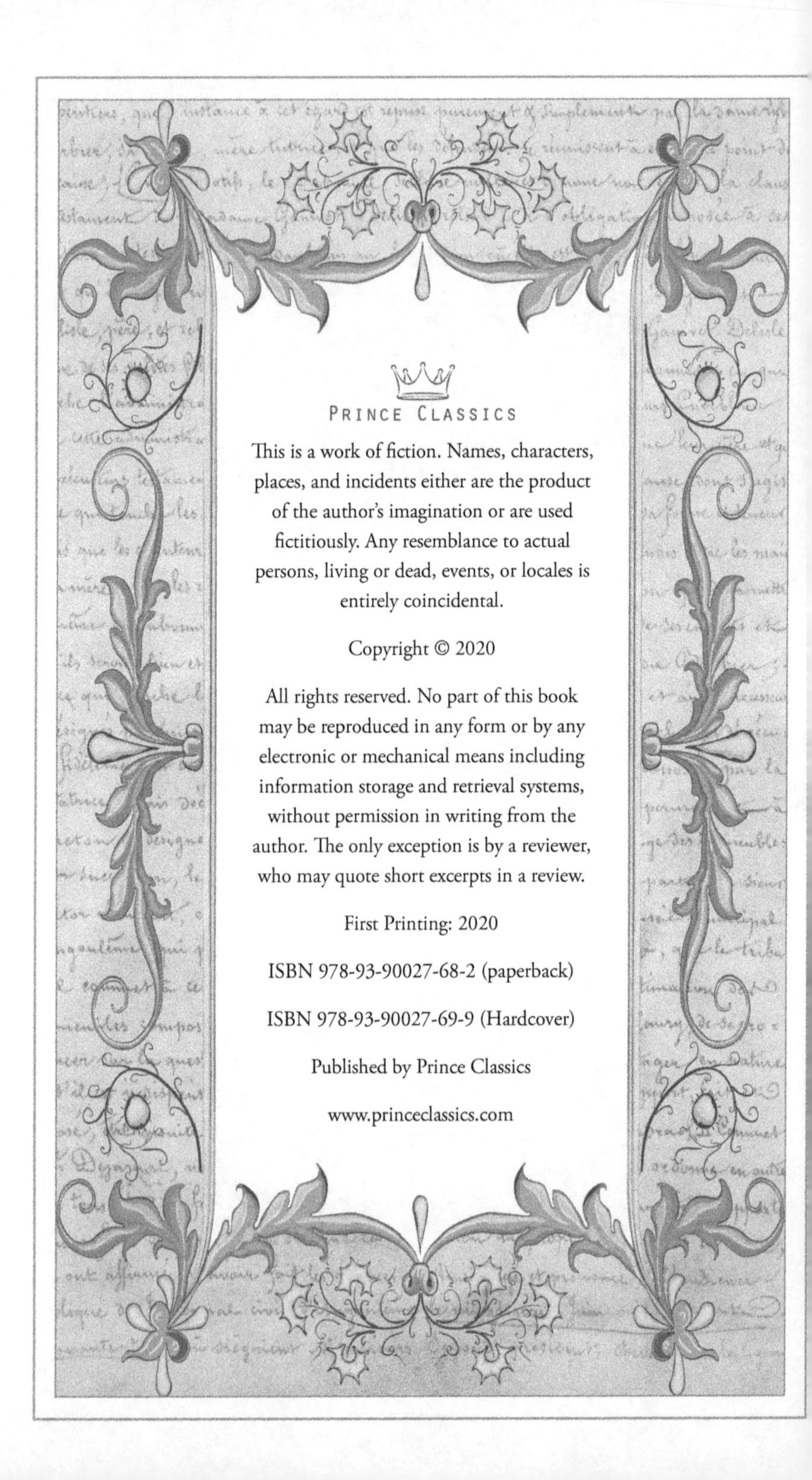

Prince Classics

First Printing: 2020

ISBN 978-93-90027-68-2 (paperback)

ISBN 978-93-90027-69-9 (Hardcover)

Published by Prince Classics

www.princeclassics.com

Contents

OTHER TALES
AND SKETCHES

MY VISIT TO NIAGARA.

Never did a pilgrim approach Niagara with deeper enthusiasm than mine. I had lingered away from it, and wandered to other scenes, because my treasury of anticipated enjoyments, comprising all the wonders of the world, had nothing else so magnificent, and I was loath to exchange the pleasures of hope for those of memory so soon. At length the day came. The stage-coach, with a Frenchman and myself on the back seat, had already left Lewiston, and in less than an hour would set us down in Manchester. I began to listen for the roar of the cataract, and trembled with a sensation like dread, as the moment drew nigh, when its voice of ages must roll, for the first time, on my ear. The French gentleman stretched himself from the window, and expressed loud admiration, while, by a sudden impulse, I threw myself back and closed my eyes. When the scene shut in, I was glad to think, that for me the whole burst of Niagara was yet in futurity. We rolled on, and entered the village of Manchester, bordering on the falls.

I am quite ashamed of myself here. Not that I ran, like a madman to the falls, and plunged into the thickest of the spray,—never stopping to breathe, till breathing was impossible: not that I committed this, or any other suitable extravagance. On the contrary, I alighted with perfect decency and composure, gave my cloak to the black waiter, pointed out my baggage, and inquired, not the nearest way to the cataract, but about the dinner-hour. The interval was spent in arranging my dress. Within the last fifteen minutes, my mind had grown strangely benumbed, and my spirits apathetic, with a slight depression, not decided enough to be termed sadness. My enthusiasm was in a deathlike slumber. Without aspiring to immortality, as he did, I could have imitated that English traveller, who turned back from the point where he first heard the thunder of Niagara, after crossing the ocean to behold it. Many a Western trader, by the by, has performed a similar act of heroism with more heroic simplicity, deeming it no such wonderful feat to dine at the hotel and resume his route to Buffalo or Lewiston, while the cataract was roaring unseen.

Such has often been my apathy, when objects, long sought, and earnestly desired, were placed within my reach. After dinner—at which an unwonted and perverse epicurism detained me longer than usual—I lighted a cigar and paced the piazza, minutely attentive to the aspect and business of a very ordinary village. Finally, with reluctant step, and the feeling of an intruder, I walked towards Goat Island. At the tollhouse, there were further excuses for delaying the inevitable moment. My signature was required in a huge ledger, containing similar records innumerable, many of which I read. The skin of a great sturgeon, and other fishes, beasts, and reptiles; a collection of minerals, such as lie in heaps near the falls; some Indian moccasins, and other trifles, made of deer-skin and embroidered with beads; several newspapers from Montreal, New York, and Boston;—all attracted me in turn. Out of a number of twisted sticks, the manufacture of a Tuscarora Indian, I selected one of curled maple, curiously convoluted, and adorned with the carved images of a snake and a fish. Using this as my pilgrim's staff, I crossed the bridge. Above and below me were the rapids, a river of impetuous snow, with here and there a dark rock amid its whiteness, resisting all the physical fury, as any cold spirit did the moral influences of the scene. On reaching Goat Island, which separates the two great segments of the falls, I chose the right-hand path, and followed it to the edge of the American cascade. There, while the falling sheet was yet invisible, I saw the vapor that never vanishes, and the Eternal Rainbow of Niagara.

It was an afternoon of glorious sunshine, without a cloud, save those of the cataracts. I gained an insulated rock, and beheld a broad sheet of brilliant and unbroken foam, not shooting in a curved line from the top of the precipice, but falling headlong down from height to depth. A narrow stream diverged from the main branch, and hurried over the crag by a channel of its own, leaving a little pine-clad island and a streak of precipice, between itself and the larger sheet. Below arose the mist, on which was painted a dazzling sun-bow with two concentric shadows,—one, almost as perfect as the original brightness; and the other, drawn faintly round the broken edge of the cloud.

Still I had not half seen Niagara. Following the verge of the island, the path led me to the Horseshoe, where the real, broad St. Lawrence, rushing along on a level with its banks, pours its whole breadth over a concave line of precipice, and thence pursues its course between lofty crags towards Ontario. A sort of bridge, two or three feet wide, stretches out along the edge of the descending sheet, and hangs upon the rising mist, as if that were the foundation of the frail structure. Here I stationed myself in the blast of wind, which the rushing river bore along with it. The bridge was tremulous beneath me, and marked the tremor of the solid earth. I looked along the whitening rapids, and endeavored to distinguish a mass of water far above the falls, to follow it to their verge, and go down with it, in fancy, to the abyss of clouds and storm. Casting my eyes across the river, and every side, I took in the whole scene at a glance, and tried to comprehend it in one vast idea. After an hour thus spent, I left the bridge, and, by a staircase, winding almost interminably round a post, descended to the base of the precipice. From that point, my path lay over slippery stones, and among great fragments of the cliff, to the edge of the cataract, where the wind at once enveloped me in spray, and perhaps dashed the rainbow round me. Were my long desires fulfilled? And had I seen Niagara?

O that I had never heard of Niagara till I beheld it! Blessed were the wanderers of old, who heard its deep roar, sounding through the woods, as the summons to an unknown wonder, and approached its awful brink, in all the freshness of native feeling. Had its own mysterious voice been the first to warn me of its existence, then, indeed, I might have knelt down and worshipped. But I had come thither, haunted with a vision of foam and fury, and dizzy cliffs, and an ocean tumbling down out of the sky,—a scene, in short, which nature had too much good taste and calm simplicity to realize. My mind had struggled to adapt these false conceptions to the reality, and finding the effort vain, a wretched sense of disappointment weighed me down. I climbed the precipice, and threw myself on the earth, feeling that I was unworthy to look at the Great Falls, and careless about beholding them again.

All that night, as there has been and will be, for ages past and to come, a rushing sound was heard, as if a great tempest were sweeping through the air. It mingled with my dreams, and made them full of storm and whirlwind. Whenever I awoke, and heard this dread sound in the air, and the windows rattling as with a mighty blast, I could not rest again, till looking forth, I saw how bright the stars were, and that every leaf in the garden was motionless. Never was a summer night more calm to the eye, nor a gale of autumn louder to the ear. The rushing sound proceeds from the rapids, and the rattling of the casements is but an effect of the vibration of the whole house, shaken by the jar of the cataract. The noise of the rapids draws the attention from the true voice of Niagara, which is a dull, muffed thunder, resounding between the cliffs. I spent a wakeful hour at midnight, in distinguishing its reverberations, and rejoiced to find that my former awe and enthusiasm were reviving.

Gradually, and after much contemplation, I came to know, by my own feelings, that Niagara is indeed a wonder of the world, and not the less wonderful, because time and thought must be employed in comprehending it. Casting aside all preconceived notions, and preparation to be dire-struck or delighted, the beholder must stand beside it in the simplicity of his heart, suffering the mighty scene to work its own impression. Night after night, I dreamed of it, and was gladdened every morning by the consciousness of a growing capacity to enjoy it. Yet I will not pretend to the all-absorbing enthusiasm of some more fortunate spectators, nor deny that very trifling causes would draw my eyes and thoughts from the cataract.

The last day that I was to spend at Niagara, before my departure for the Far West, I sat upon the Table Rock. This celebrated station did not now, as of old, project fifty feet beyond the line of the precipice, but was shattered by the fall of an immense fragment, which lay distant on the shore below. Still, on the utmost verge of the rock, with my feet hanging over it, I felt as if suspended in the open air. Never before had my mind been in such perfect unison with the scene. There were intervals, when I was conscious of nothing but the great river, rolling calmly into the abyss, rather descending than precipitating itself, and acquiring tenfold majesty from its unhurried motion. It came like the march of Destiny. It was not taken by surprise, but seemed to have anticipated, in all its course through the broad lakes, that it must pour their collected waters down this height. The perfect foam of the river, after its descent, and the ever-varying shapes of mist, rising up, to become clouds in the sky, would be the very picture of confusion, were it merely transient, like the rage of a tempest. But when the beholder has stood awhile, and perceives no lull in the storm, and considers that the vapor and the foam are as everlasting as the rocks which produce them, all this turmoil assumes a sort of calmness. It soothes, while it awes the mind.

Leaning over the cliff, I saw the guide conducting two adventurers behind the falls. It was pleasant, from that high seat in the sunshine, to observe them struggling against the eternal storm of the lower regions, with heads bent down, now faltering, now pressing forward, and finally swallowed up in their victory. After their disappearance, a blast rushed out with an old hat, which it had swept from one of their heads. The rock, to which they were directing their unseen course, is marked, at a fearful distance on the exterior of the sheet, by a jet of foam. The attempt to reach it appears both poetical and perilous to a looker-on, but may be accomplished without much more difficulty or hazard, than in stemming a violent northeaster. In a few moments, forth came the children of the mist. Dripping and breathless, they crept along the base of the cliff, ascended to the guide's cottage, and received, I presume, a certificate of their achievement, with three verses of sublime poetry on the back.

My contemplations were often interrupted by strangers, who came down from Forsyth's to take their first view of the falls. A short, ruddy, middle-aged gentleman, fresh from Old England, peeped over the rock, and evinced his approbation by a broad grin. His spouse, a very robust lady, afforded a sweet example of maternal solicitude, being so intent on the safety of her little boy that she did not even glance at Niagara. As for the child, he gave himself wholly to the enjoyment of a stick of candy. Another traveller, a native American, and no rare character among us, produced a volume of Captain Hall's tour, and labored earnestly to adjust Niagara to the captain's description, departing, at last, without one new idea or sensation of his own. The next comer was provided, not with a printed book, but with a blank sheet of foolscap, from top to bottom of which, by means of an ever-pointed pencil, the cataract was made to thunder. In a little talk, which we had together, he awarded his approbation to the general view, but censured the position of Goat Island, observing that it should have been thrown farther to the right, so as to widen the American falls, and contract those of the Horseshoe. Next appeared two traders of Michigan, who declared, that, upon the whole, the sight was worth looking at, there certainly was an immense water-power here; but that, after all, they would go twice as far to see the noble stone-works of Lockport, where the Grand Canal is locked down a descent of sixty feet. They were succeeded by a young fellow, in a homespun cotton dress, with a staff in his hand, and a pack over his shoulders. He advanced close to the edge of the rock, where his attention, at first wavering among the different components of the scene, finally became fixed in the angle of the Horse shoe falls, which is, indeed, the central point of interest. His whole soul seemed to go forth and be transported thither, till the staff slipped from his relaxed grasp, and falling down—down—down—struck upon the fragment of the Table Rock.

In this manner I spent some hours, watching the varied impression, made by the cataract, on those who disturbed me, and returning to unwearied contemplation, when left alone. At length my time came to depart. There is a grassy footpath, through the woods, along the summit of the bank, to a point whence a causeway, hewn in the side of the precipice, goes winding down to the Ferry, about half a mile below the Table Rock. The sun was near setting, when I emerged from the shadow of the trees, and began the descent. The indirectness of my downward road continually changed the point of view, and showed me, in rich and repeated succession, now, the whitening rapids and majestic leap of the main river, which appeared more deeply massive as the light departed; now, the lovelier picture, yet still sublime, of Goat Island, with its rocks and grove, and the lesser falls, tumbling over the right bank of the St. Lawrence, like a tributary stream; now, the long vista of the river, as it eddied and whirled between the cliffs, to pass through Ontario toward the sea, and everywhere to be wondered at, for this one unrivalled scene. The golden sunshine tinged the sheet of the American cascade, and painted on its heaving spray the broken semicircle of a rainbow, heaven's own beauty crowning earth's sublimity. My steps were slow, and I paused long at every turn of the descent, as one lingers and pauses, who discerns a brighter and brightening excellence in what he must soon behold no more. The solitude of the old wilderness now reigned over the whole vicinity of the falls. My enjoyment became the more rapturous, because no poet shared it, nor wretch devoid of poetry profaned it; but the spot so famous through the world was all my own!

THE ANTIQUE RING.

"Yes, indeed: the gem is as bright as a star, and curiously set," said Clara Pembertou, examining an antique ring, which her betrothed lover had just presented to her, with a very pretty speech. "It needs only one thing to make it perfect."

"And what is that?" asked Mr. Edward Caryl, secretly anxious for the credit of his gift. "A modern setting, perhaps?"

"O, no! That would destroy the charm at once," replied Clara. "It needs nothing but a story. I long to know how many times it has been the pledge of faith between two lovers, and whether the vows, of which it was the symbol, were always kept or often broken. Not that I should be too scrupulous about facts. If you happen to be unacquainted with its authentic history, so much the better. May it not have sparkled upon a queen's finger? Or who knows but it is the very ring which Posthumus received from Imogen? In short, you must kindle your imagination at the lustre of this diamond, and make a legend for it."

Now such a task—and doubtless Clara knew it—was the most acceptable that could have been imposed on Edward Caryl. He was one of that multitude of young gentlemen—limbs, or rather twigs of the law—whose names appear in gilt letters on the front of Tudor's Buildings, and other places in the vicinity of the Court House, which seem to be the haunt of the gentler as well as the severer Muses. Edward, in the dearth of clients, was accustomed to employ his much leisure in assisting the growth of American Literature, to which good cause he had contributed not a few quires of the finest letter-paper, containing some thought, some fancy, some depth of feeling, together with a young writer's abundance of conceits. Sonnets, stanzas of Tennysonian sweetness, tales imbued with German mysticism, versions from Jean Paul, criticisms of the old English poets, and essays smacking of Dialistic philosophy, were among his multifarious productions. The editors of the fashionable periodicals were familiar with his autograph, and inscribed his name in those brilliant bead-rolls of ink-stained celebrity, which illustrate the first page of their covers. Nor did fame withhold her laurel. Hillard had included him among the lights of the New England metropolis, in his Boston Book; Bryant had found room for some of his stanzas, in the Selections from American Poetry; and Mr. Griswold, in his recent assemblage of the sons and daughters of song, had introduced Edward Caryl into the inner court of the temple, among his fourscore choicest bards. There was a prospect, indeed, of his assuming a still higher and more independent position. Interviews had been held with Ticknor, and a correspondence with the Harpers, respecting a proposed volume, chiefly to consist of Mr. Caryl's fugitive pieces in the Magazines, but to be accompanied with a poem of some length, never before published. Not improbably, the public may yet be gratified with this collection.

Meanwhile, we sum up our sketch of Edward Caryl, by pronouncing him, though somewhat of a carpet knight in literature, yet no unfavorable specimen of a generation of rising writers, whose spirit is such that we may reasonably expect creditable attempts from all, and good and beautiful results from some. And, it will be observed, Edward was the very man to write pretty legends, at a lady's instance, for an old-fashioned diamond ring. He took the jewel in his hand, and turned it so as to catch its scintillating radiance, as if hoping, in accordance with Clara's suggestion, to light up his fancy with that starlike gleam.

"Shall it be a ballad?—a tale in verse?" he inquired. "Enchanted rings often glisten in old English poetry, I think something may be done with the subject; but it is fitter for rhyme than prose."

"No, no," said Miss Pemberton, "we will have no more rhyme than just enough for a posy to the ring. You must tell the legend in simple prose; and when it is finished, I will make a little party to hear it read."

The young gentleman promised obedience; and going to his pillow, with his head full of the familiar spirits that used to be worn in rings, watches, and sword-hilts, he had the good fortune to possess himself of an available idea in a dream. Connecting this with what he himself chanced to know of the ring's real history, his task was done. Clara Pemberton invited a select few of her friends, all holding the stanchest faith in Edward's genius, and therefore the most genial auditors, if not altogether the fairest critics, that a writer could possibly desire. Blessed be woman for her faculty of admiration, and especially for her tendency to admire with her heart, when man, at most, grants merely a cold approval with his mind!

Drawing his chair beneath the blaze of a solar lamp, Edward Caryl untied a roll of glossy paper, and began as follows:—

THE LEGEND

After the death-warrant had been read to the Earl of Essex, and on the evening before his appointed execution, the Countess of Shrewsbury paid his lordship a visit, and found him, as it appeared, toying childishly with a ring. The diamond, that enriched it, glittered like a little star, but with a singular tinge of red. The gloomy prison-chamber in the Tower, with its deep and narrow windows piercing the walls of stone, was now all that the earl possessed of worldly prospect; so that there was the less wonder that he should look steadfastly into the gem, and moralize upon earth's deceitful splendor, as men in darkness and ruin seldom fail to do. But the shrewd observations of the countess,—an artful and unprincipled woman,—the pretended friend of Essex, but who had come to glut her revenge for a deed of scorn which he himself had forgotten,—her keen eye detected a deeper interest attached to this jewel. Even while expressing his gratitude for her remembrance of a ruined favorite, and condemned criminal, the earl's glance reverted to the ring, as if all that remained of time and its affairs were collected within that small golden circlet.

"My dear lord," observed the countess, "there is surely some matter of great moment wherewith this ring is connected, since it, so absorbs your mind. A token, it may be, of some fair lady's love,—alas, poor lady, once richest in possessing such a heart! Would you that the jewel be returned to her?"

"The queen! the queen! It was her Majesty's own gift," replied the earl, still gazing into the depths of the gem. "She took it from her finger, and told me, with a smile, that it was an heirloom from her Tudor ancestors, and had once been the property of Merlin, the British wizard, who gave it to the lady of his love. His art had made this diamond the abiding-place of a spirit, which, though of fiendish nature, was bound to work only good, so long as the ring was an unviolated pledge of love and faith, both with the giver and receiver. But should love prove false, and faith be broken, then the evil spirit would work his own devilish will, until the ring were purified by becoming the medium of some good and holy act, and again the pledge of faithful love. The gem soon lost its virtue; for the wizard was murdered by the very lady to whom he gave it."

"An idle legend!" said the countess.

"It is so," answered Essex, with a melancholy smile. "Yet the queen's favor, of which this ring was the symbol, has proved my ruin. When death is nigh, men converse with dreams and shadows. I have been gazing into the diamond, and fancying—but you will laugh at me—that I might catch a glimpse of the evil spirit there. Do you observe this red glow,—dusky, too, amid all the brightness? It is the token of his presence; and even now, methinks, it grows redder and duskier, like an angry sunset."

Nevertheless, the earl's manner testified how slight was his credence in the enchanted properties of the ring. But there is a kind of playfulness that comes in moments of despair, when the reality of misfortune, if entirely felt, would crush the soul at once. He now, for a brief space, was lost in thought, while the countess contemplated him with malignant satisfaction.

"This ring," he resumed, in another tone, "alone remains, of all that my royal mistress's favor lavished upon her servant. My fortune once shone as brightly as the gem. And now, such a darkness has fallen around me, methinks it would be no marvel if its gleam—the sole light of my prison-house—were to be forthwith extinguished; inasmuch as my last earthly hope depends upon it."

"How say you, my lord?" asked the Countess of Shrewsbury. "The stone is bright; but there should be strange magic in it, if it can keep your hopes alive, at this sad hour. Alas! these iron bars and ramparts of the Tower are unlike to yield to such a spell."

Essex raised his head involuntarily; for there was something in the countess's tone that disturbed him, although he could not suspect that an enemy had intruded upon the sacred privacy of a prisoner's dungeon, to exult over so dark a ruin of such once brilliant fortunes. He looked her in the face, but saw nothing to awaken his distrust. It would have required a keener eye than even Cecil's to read the secret of a countenance, which had been worn so long in the false light of a court, that it was now little better than a mask, telling any story save the true one. The condemned nobleman again bent over the ring, and proceeded:

"It once had power in it,—this bright gem,—the magic that appertains to the talisman of a great queen's favor. She bade me, if hereafter I should fall into her disgrace,—how deep soever, and whatever might be the crime,—to convey this jewel to her sight, and it should plead for me. Doubtless, with her piercing judgment, she had even then detected the rashness of my nature, and foreboded some such deed as has now brought destruction upon my bead. And knowing, too, her own hereditary rigor, she designed, it may be, that the memory of gentler and kindlier hours should soften her heart in my behalf, when my need should be the greatest. I have doubted,—I have distrusted,—yet who can tell, even now, what happy influence this ring might have?"

"You have delayed full long to show the ring, and plead her Majesty's gracious promise," remarked the countess,—"your state being what it is."

"True," replied the earl: "but for my honor's sake, I was loath to entreat the queen's mercy, while I might hope for life, at least, from the justice of the laws. If, on a trial by my peers, I had been acquitted of meditating violence against her sacred life, then would I have fallen at her feet, and presenting the jewel, have prayed no other favor than that my love and zeal should be put to the severest test. But now—it were confessing too much—it were cringing too low—to beg the miserable gift of life, on no other score than the tenderness which her Majesty deems one to have forfeited!"

"Yet it is your only hope," said the countess.

"And besides," continued Essex, pursuing his own reflections, "of what avail will be this token of womanly feeling, when, on the other hand, are arrayed the all-prevailing motives of state policy, and the artifices and intrigues of courtiers, to consummate my downfall? Will Cecil or Raleigh suffer her heart to act for itself, even if the spirit of her father were not in her? It is in vain to hope it."

But still Essex gazed at the ring with an absorbed attention, that proved how much hope his sanguine temperament had concentrated here, when there was none else for him in the wide world, save what lay in the compass of that hoop of gold. The spark of brightness within the diamond, which gleamed like an intenser than earthly fire, was the memorial of his dazzling career. It had not paled with the waning sunshine of his mistress's favor; on the contrary, in spite of its remarkable tinge of dusky red, he fancied that it never shone so brightly. The glow of festal torches,—the blaze of perfumed lamps,—bonfires that had been kindled for him, when he was the darling of the people,—the splendor of the royal court, where he had been the peculiar star,—all seemed to have collected their moral or material glory into the gem, and to burn with a radiance caught from the future, as well as gathered from the past. That radiance might break forth again. Bursting from the diamond, into which it was now narrowed, it might been first upon the gloomy walls of the Tower,—then wider, wider, wider,—till all England, and the seas around her cliffs, should be gladdened with the light. It was such an ecstasy as often ensues after long depression, and has been supposed to precede the circumstances of darkest fate that may befall mortal man. The earl pressed the ring to his heart as if it were indeed a talisman, the habitation of a spirit, as the queen had playfully assured him,—but a spirit of happier influences than her legend spake of.

"O, could I but make my way to her footstool!" cried he, waving his hand aloft, while he paced the stone pavement of his prison-chamber with an impetuous step. "I might kneel down, indeed, a ruined man, condemned to the block, but how should I rise again? Once more the favorite of Elizabeth!—England's proudest noble!—with such prospects as ambition never aimed at!

Why have I tarried so long in this weary dungeon? The ring has power to set me free! The palace wants me! Ho, jailer, unbar the door!"

But then occurred the recollection of the impossibility of obtaining an interview with his fatally estranged mistress, and testing the influence over her affections, which he still flattered himself with possessing. Could he step beyond the limits of his prison, the world would be all sunshine; but here was only gloom and death.

"Alas!" said he, slowly and sadly, letting his head fall upon his hands. "I die for the lack of one blessed word."

The Countess of Shrewsbury, herself forgotten amid the earl's gorgeous visions, had watched him with an aspect that could have betrayed nothing to the most suspicious observer; unless that it was too calm for humanity, while witnessing the flutterings, as it were, of a generous heart in the death-agony. She now approached him.

"My good lord," she said, "what mean you to do?"

"Nothing,—my deeds are done!" replied he, despondingly; "yet, had a fallen favorite any friends, I would entreat one of them to lay this ring at her Majesty's feet; albeit with little hope, save that, hereafter, it might remind her that poor Essex, once far too highly favored, was at last too severely dealt with."

"I will be that friend," said the countess. "There is no time to be lost. Trust this precious ring with me. This very night the queen's eye shall rest upon it; nor shall the efficacy of my poor words be wanting, to strengthen the impression which it will doubtless make."

The earl's first impulse was to hold out the ring. But looking at the countess, as she bent forward to receive it, he fancied that the red glow of the gem tinged all her face, and gave it an ominous expression. Many passages of past times recurred to his memory. A preternatural insight, perchance caught from approaching death, threw its momentary gleam, as from a meteor, all round his position.

"Countess," he said, "I know not wherefore I hesitate, being in a plight so desperate, and having so little choice of friends. But have you looked into your own heart? Can you perform this office with the truth—the earnestness—time—zeal, even to tears, and agony of spirit—wherewith the holy gift of human life should be pleaded for? Woe be unto you, should you undertake this task, and deal towards me otherwise than with utmost faith. For your own soul's sake, and as you would have peace at your death-hour, consider well in what spirit you receive this ring!"

The countess did not shrink.

"My lord!—my good lord!" she exclaimed, "wrong not a woman's heart by these suspicious. You might choose another messenger; but who, save a lady of her bedchamber, can obtain access to the queen at this untimely hour? It is for your life,—for your life,—else I would not renew my offer."

"Take the ring," said the earl.

"Believe that it shall be in the queen's hands before the lapse of another hour," replied the countess, as she received this sacred trust of life and death. "To-morrow morning look for the result of my intercession."

She departed. Again the earl's hopes rose high. Dreams visited his slumber, not of the sable-decked scaffold in the Tower-yard, but of canopies of state, obsequious courtiers, pomp, splendor, the smile of the once more gracious queen, and a light beaming from the magic gem, which illuminated his whole future.

History records how foully the Countess of Shrewsbury betrayed the trust, which Essex, in his utmost need, confided to her. She kept the ring, and stood in the presence of Elizabeth, that night, without one attempt to soften her stern hereditary temper in behalf of the former favorite. The next day the earl's noble head rolled upon the scaffold. On her death-bed, tortured, at last, with a sense of the dreadful guilt which she had taken upon her soul, the wicked countess sent for Elizabeth, revealed the story of the ring, and besought forgiveness for her treachery. But the queen, still obdurate, even while remorse for past obduracy was tugging at her heart-strings, shook the dying woman in her bed, as if struggling with death for the privilege of wreaking her revenge and spite. The spirit of the countess passed away, to undergo the justice, or receive the mercy, of a higher tribunal; and tradition says, that the fatal ring was found upon her breast, where it had imprinted a dark red circle, resembling the effect of the intensest heat. The attendants, who prepared the body for burial, shuddered, whispering one to another, that the ring must have derived its heat from the glow of infernal fire. They left it on her breast, in the coffin, and it went with that guilty woman to the tomb.

Many years afterward, when the church, that contained the monuments of the Shrewsbury family, was desecrated by Cromwell's soldiers, they broke open the ancestral vaults, and stole whatever was valuable from the noble personages who reposed there. Merlin's antique ring passed into the possession of a stout sergeant of the Ironsides, who thus became subject to the influences of the evil spirit that still kept his abode within the gem's enchanted depths. The sergeant was soon slain in battle, thus transmitting the ring, though without any legal form of testament, to a gay cavalier, who forthwith pawned it, and expended the money in liquor, which speedily brought him to the grave. We next catch the sparkle of the magic diamond at various epochs of the merry reign of Charles the Second. But its sinister fortune still attended it. From whatever hand this ring of portent came, and whatever finger it encircled, ever it was the pledge of deceit between man and man, or man and woman, of faithless vows, and unhallowed passion; and whether to lords and ladies, or to village-maids,—for sometimes it found its way so low,—still it brought nothing but sorrow and disgrace. No purifying deed was done, to drive the fiend from his bright home in this little star. Again, we hear of it at a later period, when Sir Robert Walpole bestowed the ring, among far richer jewels, on the lady of a British legislator, whose political honor he wished to undermine. Many a dismal and unhappy tale might be wrought out of its other adventures. All this while, its ominous tinge of dusky red had been deepening and darkening, until, if laid upon white paper, it cast the mingled hue of night and blood, strangely illuminated with scintillating light, in a circle round about. But this peculiarity only made it the more valuable.

Alas, the fatal ring! When shall its dark secret be discovered, and the doom of ill, inherited from one possessor to another, be finally revoked?

The legend now crosses the Atlantic, and comes down to our own immediate time. In a certain church of our city, not many evenings ago, there was a contribution for a charitable object. A fervid preacher had poured out his whole soul in a rich and tender discourse, which had at least excited the tears, and perhaps the more effectual sympathy, of a numerous audience. While the choristers sang sweetly, and the organ poured forth its melodious thunder, the deacons passed up and down the aisles, and along the galleries, presenting their mahogany boxes, in which each person deposited whatever sum he deemed it safe to lend to the Lord, in aid of human wretchedness. Charity became audible,—chink, chink, chink,—as it fell, drop by drop, into the common receptacle. There was a hum,—a stir,—the subdued bustle of people putting their hands into their pockets; while, ever and anon, a vagrant coin fell upon the floor, and rolled away, with long reverberation, into some inscrutable corner.

At length, all having been favored with an opportunity to be generous, the two deacons placed their boxes on the communion-table, and thence, at the conclusion of the services, removed them into the vestry. Here these good old gentlemen sat down together, to reckon the accumulated treasure.

"Fie, fie, Brother Tilton," said Deacon Trott, peeping into Deacon Tilton's box, "what a heap of copper you have picked up! Really, for an old man, you must have had a heavy job to lug it along. Copper! copper! copper! Do people expect to get admittance into heaven at the price of a few coppers?"

"Don't wrong them, brother," answered Deacon Tilton, a simple and kindly old man. "Copper may do more for one person, than gold will for another. In the galleries, where I present my box, we must not expect such a harvest as you gather among the gentry in the broad aisle, and all over the floor of the church. My people are chiefly poor mechanics and laborers, sailors, seamstresses, and servant-maids, with a most uncomfortable intermixture of roguish school-boys."

"Well, well," said Deacon Trott; "but there is a great deal, Brother Tilton, in the method of presenting a contribution-box. It is a knack that comes by nature, or not at all."

They now proceeded to sum up the avails of the evening, beginning with the receipts of Deacon Trott. In good sooth, that worthy personage had reaped an abundant harvest, in which he prided himself no less, apparently, than if every dollar had been contributed from his own individual pocket. Had the good deacon been meditating a jaunt to Texas, the treasures of the mahogany box might have sent him on his way rejoicing. There were bank-notes, mostly, it is true, of the smallest denominations in the giver's pocket-book, yet making a goodly average upon the whole. The most splendid contribution was a check for a hundred dollars, bearing the name of a distinguished merchant, whose liberality was duly celebrated in the newspapers of the next day. No less than seven half-eagles, together with an English sovereign, glittered amidst an indiscriminate heap of silver; the box being polluted with nothing of the copper kind, except a single bright new cent, wherewith a little boy had performed his first charitable act.

"Very well! very well indeed!" said Deacon Trott, self-approvingly. "A handsome evening's work! And now, Brother Tilton, let's see whether you can match it." Here was a sad contrast! They poured forth Deacon Tilton's treasure upon the table, and it really seemed as if the whole copper coinage of the country, together with an amazing quantity of shop-keeper's tokens, and English and Irish half-pence, mostly of base metal, had been congregated into the box. There was a very substantial pencil-case, and the semblance of a shilling; but he latter proved to be made of tin, and the former of German-silver. A gilded brass button was doing duty as a gold coin, and a folded shopbill had assumed the character of a bank-note. But Deacon Tilton's feelings were much revived by the aspect of another bank-note, new and crisp, adorned with beautiful engravings, and stamped with the indubitable word, TWENTY, in large black letters. Alas! it was a counterfeit. In short, the poor old Deacon was no less unfortunate than those who trade with fairies, and whose gains are sure to be transformed into dried leaves, pebbles, and other valuables of that kind.

"I believe the Evil One is in the box," said he, with some vexation.

"Well done, Deacon Tilton!" cried his Brother Trott, with a hearty laugh. "You ought to have a statue in copper."

"Never mind, brother," replied the good Deacon, recovering his temper. "I'll bestow ten dollars from my own pocket, and may heaven's blessing go along with it. But look! what do you call this?"

Under the copper mountain, which it had cost them so much toil to remove, lay an antique ring! It was enriched with a diamond, which, so soon as it caught the light, began to twinkle and glimmer, emitting the whitest and purest lustre that could possibly be conceived.—It was as brilliant as if some magician had condensed the brightest star in heaven into a compass fit to be set in a ring, for a lady's delicate finger.

"How is this?" said Deacon Trott, examining it carefully, in the expectation of finding it as worthless as the rest of his colleague's treasure. "Why, upon my word, this seems to be a real diamond, and of the purest water. Whence could it have come?"

"Really, I cannot tell," quoth Deacon Tilton, "for my spectacles were so misty that all faces looked alike. But now I remember, there was a flash of light came from the box, at one moment; but it seemed a dusky red, instead of a pure white, like the sparkle of this gem. Well; the ring will make up for the copper; but I wish the giver had thrown its history into the box along with it."

It has been our good luck to recover a portion of that history. After transmitting misfortune from one possessor to another, ever since the days of British Merlin, the identical ring which Queen Elizabeth gave to the Earl of Essex was finally thrown into the contribution-box of a New England church. The two deacons deposited it in the glass case of a fashionable jeweller, of whom it was purchased by the humble rehearser of this legend, in the hope that it may be allowed to sparkle on a fair lady's finger. Purified from the foul fiend, so long its inhabitant, by a deed of unostentatious charity, and now made the symbol of faithful and devoted love, the gentle bosom of its new possessor need fear no sorrow from its influence.

Very pretty!—Beautiful!—How original!—How sweetly written!—What nature!—What imagination!—What power!—What pathos!—What exquisite humor!"—were the exclamations of Edward Caryl's kind and generous auditors, at the conclusion of the legend.

"It is a pretty tale," said Miss Pemberton, who, conscious that her praise was to that of all others as a diamond to a pebble, was therefore the less liberal in awarding it. "It is really a pretty tale, and very proper for any of the Annuals. But, Edward, your moral does not satisfy me. What thought did you embody in the ring?"

"O Clara, this is too bad!" replied Edward, with a half-reproachful smile. "You know that I can never separate the idea from the symbol in which it manifests itself. However, we may suppose the Gem to be the human heart, and the Evil Spirit to be Falsehood, which, in one guise or another, is the fiend that causes all the sorrow and trouble in the world. I beseech you to let this suffice."

"It shall," said Clara, kindly. "And, believe me, whatever the world may say of the story, I prize it far above the diamond which enkindled your imagination."

GRAVES AND GOBLINS.

Now talk we of graves and goblins! Fit themes,—start not! gentle reader,—fit for a ghost like me. Yes; though an earth-clogged fancy is laboring with these conceptions, and an earthly hand will write them down, for mortal eyes to read, still their essence flows from as airy a ghost as ever basked in the pale starlight, at twelve o'clock. Judge them not by the gross and heavy form in which they now appear. They may be gross, indeed, with the earthly pollution contracted from the brain, through which they pass; and heavy with the burden of mortal language, that crushes all the finer intelligences of the soul. This is no fault of mine. But should aught of ethereal spirit be perceptible, yet scarcely so, glimmering along the dull train of words,—should a faint perfume breathe from the mass of clay,—then, gentle reader, thank the ghost, who thus embodies himself for your sake! Will you believe me, if I say that all true and noble thoughts, and elevated imaginations, are but partly the offspring of the intellect which seems to produce them? Sprites, that were poets once, and are now all poetry, hover round the dreaming bard, and become his inspiration; buried statesmen lend their wisdom, gathered on earth and mellowed in the grave, to the historian; and when the preacher rises nearest to the level of his mighty subject, it is because the prophets of old days have communed with him. Who has not been conscious of mysteries within his mind, mysteries of truth and reality, which will not wear the chains of language? Mortal, then the dead were with you! And thus shall the earth-dulled soul, whom I inspire, be conscious of a misty brightness among his thoughts, and strive to make it gleam upon the page,—but all in vain. Poor author! How will he despise what he can grasp, for the sake of the dim glory that eludes him!

So talk we of graves and goblins. But, what have ghosts to do with graves? Mortal man, wearing the dust which shall require a sepulchre, might deem it more a home and resting-place than a spirit can, whose earthly clod has returned to earth. Thus philosophers have reasoned. Yet wiser they who adhere to the ancient sentiment, that a phantom haunts and hallows the marble tomb or grassy hillock where its material form was laid. Till purified from each stain of clay; till the passions of the living world are all forgotten; till it have less brotherhood with the wayfarers of earth, than with spirits that never wore mortality,—the ghost must linger round the grave. O, it is a long and dreary watch to some of us!

Even in early childhood, I had selected a sweet spot, of shade and glimmering sunshine, for my grave. It was no burial-ground, but a secluded nook of virgin earth, where I used to sit, whole summer afternoons, dreaming about life and death. My fancy ripened prematurely, and taught me secrets which I could not otherwise have known. I pictured the coming years,—they never came to me, indeed; but I pictured them like life, and made this spot the scene of all that should be brightest, in youth, manhood, and old age. There, in a little while, it would be time for me to breathe the bashful and burning vows of first-love; thither, after gathering fame abroad, I would return to enjoy the loud plaudit of the world, a vast but unobtrusive sound, like the booming of a distant sea; and thither, at the far-off close of life, an aged man would come, to dream, as the boy was dreaming, and be as happy in the past as lie was in futurity. Finally, when all should be finished, in that spot so hallowed, in that soil so impregnated with the most precious of my bliss, there was to be my grave. Methought it would be the sweetest grave that ever a mortal frame reposed in, or an ethereal spirit haunted. There, too, in future times, drawn thither by the spell which I had breathed around the place, boyhood would sport and dream, and youth would love, and manhood would enjoy, and age would dream again, and my ghost would watch but never frighten them. Alas, the vanity of mortal projects, even when they centre in the grave! I died in my first youth, before I had been a lover; at a distance, also, from the grave which fancy had dug for me; and they buried me in the thronged cemetery of a town, where my marble slab stands unnoticed amid a hundred others. And there are coffins on each side of mine!

"Alas, poor ghost!" will the reader say. Yet I am a happy ghost enough, and disposed to be contented with my grave, if the sexton will but let it be my own, and bring no other dead man to dispute my title. Earth has left few stains upon me, and it will be but a short time that I need haunt the place. It is good to die in early youth. Had I lived out threescore years and ten, or half of them, my spirit would have been so earth-incrusted, that centuries might not have purified it for a better home than the dark precincts of the grave. Meantime, there is good choice of company amongst us. From twilight till near sunrise, we are gliding to and fro, some in the graveyard, others miles away; and would we speak with any friend, we do but knock against his tombstone, and pronounce the name engraved on it: in an instant, there the shadow stands!

Some are ghosts of considerable antiquity. There is an old man, hereabout; he never had a tombstone, and is often puzzled to distinguish his own grave; but hereabouts he haunts, and long is doomed to haunt. He was a miser in his lifetime, and buried a strong box of ill-gotten gold, almost fresh from the mint, in the coinage of William and Mary. Scarcely was it safe, when the sexton buried the old man and his secret with him. I could point out the place where the treasure lies; it was at the bottom of the miser's garden; but a paved thoroughfare now passes beside the spot, and the cornerstone of a market-house presses right down upon it. Had the workmen dug six inches deeper, they would have found the hoard. Now thither must this poor old miser go, whether in starlight, moonshine, or pitch darkness, and brood above his worthless treasure, recalling all the petty crimes by which he gained it. Not a coin must he fail to reckon in his memory, nor forget a pennyworth of the sin that made up the sum, though his agony is such as if the pieces of gold, red-hot, were stamped into his naked soul. Often, while he is in torment there, he hears the steps of living men, who love the dross of earth as well as he did. May they never groan over their miserable wealth like him! Night after night, for above a hundred years, hath he done this penance, and still must he do it, till the iron box be brought to light, and each separate coin be cleansed by grateful tears of a widow or an orphan. My spirit sighs for his long vigil at the corner of the market-house!

There are ghosts whom I tremble to meet, and cannot think of without a shudder. One has the guilt of blood upon him. The soul which he thrust untimely forth has long since been summoned from our gloomy graveyard, and dwells among the stars of heaven, too far and too high for even the recollection of mortal anguish to ascend thither. Not so the murderer's ghost! It is his doom to spend all the hours of darkness in the spot which he stained with innocent blood, and to feel the hot stream—hot as when it first gushed upon his hand—incorporating itself with his spiritual substance. Thus his horrible crime is ever fresh within him. Two other wretches are condemned to walk arm in arm. They were guilty lovers in their lives, and still, in death, must wear the guise of love, though hatred and loathing have become their very nature and existence. The pollution of their mutual sin remains with them, and makes their souls sick continually. O, that I might forget all the dark shadows which haunt about these graves! This passing thought of them has left a stain, and will weigh me down among dust and sorrow, beyond the time that my own transgressions would have kept me here. There is one shade among us, whose high nature it is good to meditate upon. He lived a patriot, and is a patriot still. Posterity has forgotten him. The simple slab, of red freestone, that bore his name, was broken long ago, and is now covered by the gradual accumulation of the soil. A tuft of thistles is his only monument. This upright spirit came to his grave, after a lengthened life, with so little stain of earth, that he might, almost immediately, have trodden the pathway of the sky. But his strong love of country chained him down, to share its vicissitudes of weal or woe. With such deep yearning in his soul, he was unfit for heaven. That noblest virtue has the effect of sin, and keeps his pure and lofty spirit in a penance, which may not terminate till America be again a wilderness. Not that there is no joy for the dead patriot. Can he fail to experience it, while be contemplates the mighty and increasing power of the land, which be protected in its infancy? No; there is much to gladden him. But sometimes I dread to meet him, as he returns from the bedchambers of rulers and politicians, after diving into their secret motives, and searching out their aims. He looks round him with a stern and awful sadness, and vanishes into his neglected grave. Let nothing sordid or selfish defile your deeds or thoughts, ye great men of the day, lest ye grieve the noble dead.

Few ghosts take such an endearing interest as this, even in their own private affairs. It made me rather sad, at first, to find how soon the flame of love expires amid the chill damps of the tomb; so much the sooner, the more fiercely it may have burned. Forget your dead mistress, youth! She has already forgotten you. Maiden, cease to weep for your buried lover! He will know nothing of your tears, nor value them if he did. Yet it were blasphemy to say that true love is other than immortal. It is an earthly passion, of which I speak, mingled with little that is spiritual, and must therefore perish with the perishing clay. When souls have loved, there is no falsehood or forgetfulness. Maternal affection, too, is strong as adamant. There are mothers here, among us, who might have been in heaven fifty years ago, if they could forbear to cherish earthly joy and sorrow, reflected from the bosoms of their children. Husbands and wives have a comfortable gift of oblivion, especially when secure of the faith of their living halves. Jealousy, it is true, will play the devil with a ghost, driving him to the bedside of secondary wedlock, there to scowl, unseen, and gibber inaudible remonstrances. Dead wives, however jealous in their lifetime, seldom feel this posthumous torment so acutely.

Many, many things, that appear most important while we walk the busy street, lose all their interest the moment we are borne into the quiet graveyard which borders it. For my own part, my spirit had not become so mixed up with earthly existence, as to be now held in an unnatural combination, or tortured much with retrospective cares. I still love my parents and a younger sister, who remain among the living, and often grieve me by their patient sorrow for the dead. Each separate tear of theirs is an added weight upon my soul, and lengthens my stay among the graves. As to other matters, it exceedingly rejoices me, that my summons came before I had time to write a projected poem, which was highly imaginative in conception, and could not have failed to give me a triumphant rank in the choir of our native bards. Nothing is so much to be deprecated as posthumous renown. It keeps the immortal spirit from the proper bliss of his celestial state, and causes him to feed upon the impure breath of mortal man, till sometimes he forgets that there are starry realms above him. Few poets—infatuated that they are!—soar upward while the least whisper of their name is heard on earth. On Sabbath evenings, my sisters sit by the fireside, between our father and mother, and repeat some hymns of mine, which they have often heard from my own lips, ere the tremulous voice left them forever. Little do they think, those dear ones, that the dead stands listening in the glimmer of the firelight, and is almost gifted with a visible shape by the fond intensity of their remembrance.

Now shall the reader know a grief of the poor ghost that speaks to him; a grief, but not a helpless one. Since I have dwelt among the graves, they bore the corpse of a young maiden hither, and laid her in the old ancestral vault, which is hollowed in the side of a grassy bank. It has a door of stone, with rusty iron hinges, and above it, a rude sculpture of the family arms, and inscriptions of all their names who have been buried there, including sire and son, mother and daughter, of an ancient colonial race. All of her lineage had gone before, and when the young maiden followed, the portal was closed forever. The night after her burial, when the other ghosts were flitting about their graves, forth came the pale virgin's shadow, with the rest, but knew not whither to go, nor whom to haunt, so lonesome had she been on earth. She stood by the ancient sepulchre, looking upward to the bright stars, as if she would, even then, begin her flight. Her sadness made me sad. That night and the next, I stood near her, in the moonshine, but dared not speak, because she seemed purer than all the ghosts, and fitter to converse with angels than with men. But the third bright eve, still gazing upward to the glory of the heavens, she sighed, and said, "When will my mother come for me?" Her low, sweet voice emboldened me to speak, and she was kind and gentle, though so pure, and answered me again. From that time, always at the ghostly hour, I sought the old tomb of her fathers, and either found her standing by the door, or knocked, and she appeared. Blessed creature, that she was; her chaste spirit hallowed mine, and imparted such a celestial buoyancy, that I longed to grasp her hand, and fly,—upward, aloft, aloft! I thought, too, that she only lingered here, till my earthlier soul should be purified for heaven. One night, when the stars threw down the light that shadows love, I stole forth to the accustomed spot, and knocked, with my airy fingers, at her door. She answered not. Again I knocked, and breathed her name. Where was she? At once, the truth fell on my miserable spirit, and crushed it to the earth, among dead men's bones and mouldering dust, groaning in cold and desolate agony. Her penance was over! She had taken her trackless flight, and had found a home in the purest radiance of the upper stars, leaving me to knock at the stone portal of the darksome sepulchre. But I know—I know, that angels hurried her away, or surely she would have whispered ere she fled!

She is gone! How could the grave imprison that unspotted one! But her pure, ethereal spirit will not quite forget me, nor soar too high in bliss, till I ascend to join her. Soon, soon be that hour! I am weary of the earth-damps; they burden me; they choke me! Already, I can float in the moonshine; the faint starlight will almost bear up my footsteps; the perfume of flowers, which grosser spirits love, is now too earthly a luxury for me. Grave! Grave! thou art not my home. I must flit a little longer in thy night gloom, and then be gone,—far from the dust of the living and the dead,—far from the corruption that is around me, but no more within!

A few times, I have visited the chamber of one who walks, obscure and lonely, on his mortal pilgrimage. He will leave not many living friends, when he goes to join the dead, where his thoughts often stray, and he might better be. I steal into his sleep, and play my part among the figures of his dreams. I glide through the moonlight of his waking fancy, and whisper conceptions, which, with a strange thrill of fear, he writes down as his own. I stand beside him now, at midnight, telling these dreamy truths with a voice so dream-like, that he mistakes them for fictions of a brain too prone to such. Yet he glances behind him and shivers, while the lamp burns pale. Farewell, dreamer,—waking or sleeping! Your brightest dreams are fled; your mind grows too hard and cold for a spiritual guest to enter; you are earthly, too, and have all the sins of earth. The ghost will visit you no more.

But where is the maiden, holy and pure, though wearing a form of clay, that would have me bend over her pillow at midnight, and leave a blessing there? With a silent invocation, let her summon me. Shrink not, maiden, when I come! In life, I was a high-souled youth, meditative, yet seldom sad, full of chaste fancies, and stainless from all grosser sin. And now, ill death, I bring no loathsome smell of the grave, nor ghostly terrors,—but gentle, and soothing, and sweetly pensive influences. Perhaps, just fluttering for the skies, my visit may hallow the wellsprings of thy thought, and make thee heavenly here on earth. Then shall pure dreams and holy meditations bless thy life; nor thy sainted spirit linger round the grave, but seek the upper stars, and meet me there!

About Author

Nathaniel Hawthorne (**Hathorne**; July 4, 1804 – May 19, 1864) was an American novelist, dark romantic, and short story writer. His works often focus on history, morality, and religion.

He was born in 1804 in Salem, Massachusetts, to Nathaniel Hathorne and the former Elizabeth Clarke Manning. His ancestors include John Hathorne, the only judge involved in the Salem witch trials who never repented of his actions. He entered Bowdoin College in 1821, was elected to Phi Beta Kappa in 1824, and graduated in 1825. He published his first work in 1828, the novel Fanshawe; he later tried to suppress it, feeling that it was not equal to the standard of his later work. He published several short stories in periodicals, which he collected in 1837 as Twice-Told Tales. The next year, he became engaged to Sophia Peabody. He worked at the Boston Custom House and joined Brook Farm, a transcendentalist community, before marrying Peabody in 1842. The couple moved to The Old Manse in Concord, Massachusetts, later moving to Salem, the Berkshires, then to The Wayside in Concord. The Scarlet Letter was published in 1850, followed by a succession of other novels. A political appointment as consul took Hawthorne and family to Europe before their return to Concord in 1860. Hawthorne died on May 19, 1864, and was survived by his wife and their three children.

Much of Hawthorne's writing centers on New England, many works featuring moral metaphors with an anti-Puritan inspiration. His fiction works are considered part of the Romantic movement and, more specifically, dark romanticism. His themes often center on the inherent evil and sin of humanity, and his works often have moral messages and deep psychological complexity. His published works include novels, short stories, and a biography of his college friend Franklin Pierce, the 14th President of the United States.

Biography

Early life

Nathaniel Hawthorne was born on July 4, 1804, in Salem, Massachusetts;

his birthplace is preserved and open to the public. William Hathorne was the author's great-great-great-grandfather. He was a Puritan and was the first of the family to emigrate from England, settling in Dorchester, Massachusetts, before moving to Salem. There he became an important member of the Massachusetts Bay Colony and held many political positions, including magistrate and judge, becoming infamous for his harsh sentencing. William's son and the author's great-great-grandfather John Hathorne was one of the judges who oversaw the Salem witch trials. Hawthorne probably added the "w" to his surname in his early twenties, shortly after graduating from college, in an effort to dissociate himself from his notorious forebears. Hawthorne's father Nathaniel Hathorne Sr. was a sea captain who died in 1808 of yellow fever in Suriname; he had been a member of the East India Marine Society. After his death, his widow moved with young Nathaniel and two daughters to live with relatives named the Mannings in Salem, where they lived for 10 years. Young Hawthorne was hit on the leg while playing "bat and ball" on November 10, 1813, and he became lame and bedridden for a year, though several physicians could find nothing wrong with him.

In the summer of 1816, the family lived as boarders with farmers before moving to a home recently built specifically for them by Hawthorne's uncles Richard and Robert Manning in Raymond, Maine, near Sebago Lake. Years later, Hawthorne looked back at his time in Maine fondly: "Those were delightful days, for that part of the country was wild then, with only scattered clearings, and nine tenths of it primeval woods." In 1819, he was sent back to Salem for school and soon complained of homesickness and being too far from his mother and sisters. He distributed seven issues of The Spectator to his family in August and September 1820 for the sake of having fun. The homemade newspaper was written by hand and included essays, poems, and news featuring the young author's adolescent humor.

Hawthorne's uncle Robert Manning insisted that the boy attend college, despite Hawthorne's protests. With the financial support of his uncle, Hawthorne was sent to Bowdoin College in 1821, partly because of family connections in the area, and also because of its relatively inexpensive tuition rate. Hawthorne met future president Franklin Pierce on the way to

Bowdoin, at the stage stop in Portland, and the two became fast friends. Once at the school, he also met future poet Henry Wadsworth Longfellow, future congressman Jonathan Cilley, and future naval reformer Horatio Bridge. He graduated with the class of 1825, and later described his college experience to Richard Henry Stoddard:

> I was educated (as the phrase is) at Bowdoin College. I was an idle student, negligent of college rules and the Procrustean details of academic life, rather choosing to nurse my own fancies than to dig into Greek roots and be numbered among the learned Thebans.

Early career

In 1836, Hawthorne served as the editor of the American Magazine of Useful and Entertaining Knowledge. At the time, he boarded with poet Thomas Green Fessenden on Hancock Street in Beacon Hill in Boston. He was offered an appointment as weigher and gauger at the Boston Custom House at a salary of $1,500 a year, which he accepted on January 17, 1839. During his time there, he rented a room from George Stillman Hillard, business partner of Charles Sumner. Hawthorne wrote in the comparative obscurity of what he called his "owl's nest" in the family home. As he looked back on this period of his life, he wrote: "I have not lived, but only dreamed about living." He contributed short stories to various magazines and annuals, including "Young Goodman Brown" and "The Minister's Black Veil", though none drew major attention to him. Horatio Bridge offered to cover the risk of collecting these stories in the spring of 1837 into the volume Twice-Told Tales, which made Hawthorne known locally.

Marriage and family

While at Bowdoin, Hawthorne wagered a bottle of Madeira wine with his friend Jonathan Cilley that Cilley would get married before Hawthorne did. By 1836, he had won the bet, but he did not remain a bachelor for life. He had public flirtations with Mary Silsbee and Elizabeth Peabody, then he began pursuing Peabody's sister, illustrator and transcendentalist Sophia Peabody. He joined the transcendentalist Utopian community at Brook Farm in 1841, not because he agreed with the experiment but because it helped him save money to marry Sophia. He paid a $1,000 deposit and was put in charge of shoveling the hill of manure referred to as "the Gold Mine". He left later that year, though his Brook Farm adventure became an inspiration for his novel The Blithedale Romance. Hawthorne married Sophia Peabody on July 9, 1842, at a ceremony in the Peabody parlor on West Street in Boston. The couple moved to The Old Manse in Concord, Massachusetts, where they lived for three years. His neighbor Ralph Waldo Emerson invited him into his social circle, but Hawthorne was almost pathologically shy and stayed silent at gatherings. At the Old Manse, Hawthorne wrote most of the tales collected in Mosses from an Old Manse.

Like Hawthorne, Sophia was a reclusive person. Throughout her early life, she had frequent migraines and underwent several experimental medical treatments. She was mostly bedridden until her sister introduced her to Hawthorne, after which her headaches seem to have abated. The Hawthornes enjoyed a long and happy marriage. He referred to her as his "Dove" and wrote that she "is, in the strictest sense, my sole companion; and I need no other—there is no vacancy in my mind, any more than in my heart ... Thank God that I suffice for her boundless heart!" Sophia greatly admired her husband's work. She wrote in one of her journals:

> I am always so dazzled and bewildered with the richness, the depth, the ... jewels of beauty in his productions that I am always looking forward to a second reading where I can ponder and muse and fully take in the miraculous wealth of thoughts.

Poet Ellery Channing came to the Old Manse for help on the first anniversary of the Hawthornes' marriage. A local teenager named Martha Hunt had drowned herself in the river and Hawthorne's boat Pond Lily was needed to find her body. Hawthorne helped recover the corpse, which he described as "a spectacle of such perfect horror ... She was the very image of death-agony". The incident later inspired a scene in his novel The Blithedale Romance.

The Hawthornes had three children. Their first was daughter Una, born March 3, 1844; her name was a reference to The Faerie Queene, to the displeasure of family members. Hawthorne wrote to a friend, "I find it a very sober and serious kind of happiness that springs from the birth of a child ... There is no escaping it any longer. I have business on earth now, and must look about me for the means of doing it." In October 1845, the Hawthornes moved to Salem. In 1846, their son Julian was born. Hawthorne wrote to his sister Louisa on June 22, 1846: "A small troglodyte made his appearance here at ten minutes to six o'clock this morning, who claimed to be your nephew." Daughter Rose was born in May 1851, and Hawthorne called her his "autumnal flower".

Middle years

In April 1846, Hawthorne was officially appointed the Surveyor for the District of Salem and Beverly and Inspector of the Revenue for the Port of Salem at an annual salary of $1,200. He had difficulty writing during this period, as he admitted to Longfellow:

> I am trying to resume my pen ... Whenever I sit alone, or walk alone, I find myself dreaming about stories, as of old; but these forenoons in the Custom House undo all that the afternoons and evenings have done. I should be happier if I could write.

This employment, like his earlier appointment to the custom house in Boston, was vulnerable to the politics of the spoils system. Hawthorne was a Democrat and lost this job due to the change of administration in Washington after the presidential election of 1848. He wrote a letter of protest to the Boston Daily Advertiser which was attacked by the Whigs and supported by the Democrats, making Hawthorne's dismissal a much-talked about event in New England. He was deeply affected by the death of his mother in late July, calling it "the darkest hour I ever lived". He was appointed the corresponding secretary of the Salem Lyceum in 1848. Guests who came to speak that season included Emerson, Thoreau, Louis Agassiz, and Theodore Parker.

Hawthorne returned to writing and published The Scarlet Letter in mid-March 1850, including a preface that refers to his three-year tenure in the Custom House and makes several allusions to local politicians—who did not appreciate their treatment. It was one of the first mass-produced books in America, selling 2,500 volumes within ten days and earning Hawthorne $1,500 over 14 years. The book was pirated by booksellers in London and became a best-seller in the United States; it initiated his most lucrative period as a writer. Hawthorne's friend Edwin Percy Whipple objected to the novel's "morbid intensity" and its dense psychological details, writing that the book "is therefore apt to become, like Hawthorne, too painfully anatomical in his exhibition of them", though 20th-century writer D. H. Lawrence said that there could be no more perfect work of the American imagination than The Scarlet Letter.

Hawthorne and his family moved to a small red farmhouse near Lenox, Massachusetts, at the end of March 1850. He became friends with Herman Melville beginning on August 5, 1850, when the authors met at a picnic hosted by a mutual friend. Melville had just read Hawthorne's short story collection Mosses from an Old Manse, and his unsigned review of the collection was printed in The Literary World on August 17 and August 24 titled "Hawthorne and His Mosses". Melville wrote that these stories revealed a dark side to Hawthorne, "shrouded in blackness, ten times black". He was composing his novel Moby-Dick at the time, and dedicated the work in 1851 to Hawthorne: "In token of my admiration for his genius, this book is inscribed to Nathaniel Hawthorne."

Hawthorne's time in the Berkshires was very productive. While there, he wrote The House of the Seven Gables (1851), which poet and critic James Russell Lowell said was better than The Scarlet Letter and called "the most valuable contribution to New England history that has been made." He also wrote The Blithedale Romance (1852), his only work written in the first person. He also published A Wonder-Book for Girls and Boys in 1851, a collection of short stories retelling myths which he had been thinking about writing since 1846. Nevertheless, poet Ellery Channing reported that Hawthorne "has suffered much living in this place". The family enjoyed the scenery of the Berkshires, although Hawthorne did not enjoy the winters in their small house. They left on November 21, 1851. Hawthorne noted, "I am sick to death of Berkshire ... I have felt languid and dispirited, during almost my whole residence."

The Wayside and Europe

In May 1852, the Hawthornes returned to Concord where they lived until July 1853. In February, they bought The Hillside, a home previously inhabited by Amos Bronson Alcott and his family, and renamed it The Wayside. Their neighbors in Concord included Emerson and Henry David Thoreau.That year, Hawthorne wrote The Life of Franklin Pierce, the campaign biography of his friend which depicted him as "a man of peaceful pursuits". Horace Mann said, "If he makes out Pierce to be a great man or a brave man, it will be the greatest work of fiction he ever wrote." In the biography, Hawthorne depicts Pierce as a statesman and soldier who had accomplished no great feats because of his need to make "little noise" and so "withdrew into the background". He also left out Pierce's drinking habits, despite rumors of his alcoholism, and emphasized Pierce's belief that slavery could not "be remedied by human contrivances" but would, over time, "vanish like a dream".

With Pierce's election as President, Hawthorne was rewarded in 1853 with the position of United States consul in Liverpool shortly after the publication of Tanglewood Tales.The role was considered the most lucrative foreign service position at the time, described by Hawthorne's wife as "second in dignity to the Embassy in London". His appointment ended in 1857 at the close of the Pierce administration, and the Hawthorne family toured France and Italy. During his time in Italy, the previously clean-shaven Hawthorne grew a bushy mustache.

The family returned to The Wayside in 1860, and that year saw the publication of The Marble Faun, his first new book in seven years. Hawthorne admitted that he had aged considerably, referring to himself as "wrinkled with time and trouble".

Later years and death

At the outset of the American Civil War, Hawthorne traveled with William D. Ticknor to Washington, D.C., where he met Abraham Lincoln and other notable figures. He wrote about his experiences in the essay "Chiefly About War Matters" in 1862.

Failing health prevented him from completing several more romance novels. Hawthorne was suffering from pain in his stomach and insisted on a recuperative trip with his friend Franklin Pierce, though his neighbor Bronson Alcott was concerned that Hawthorne was too ill. While on a tour of the White Mountains, he died in his sleep on May 19, 1864, in Plymouth, New Hampshire. Pierce sent a telegram to Elizabeth Peabody asking her to inform Mrs. Hawthorne in person. Mrs. Hawthorne was too saddened by the news to handle the funeral arrangements herself. Hawthorne's son Julian was a freshman at Harvard College, and he learned of his father's death the next day; coincidentally, he was initiated into the Delta Kappa Epsilon fraternity on the same day by being blindfolded and placed in a coffin.Longfellow wrote a tribute poem to Hawthorne published in 1866 called "The Bells of Lynn". Hawthorne was buried on what is now known as "Authors' Ridge" in Sleepy Hollow Cemetery, Concord, Massachusetts. Pallbearers included Longfellow, Emerson, Alcott, Oliver Wendell Holmes Sr., James Thomas Fields, and Edwin Percy Whipple. Emerson wrote of the funeral: "I thought there was a tragic element in the event, that might be more fully rendered—in the painful solitude of the man, which, I suppose, could no longer be endured, & he died of it."

His wife Sophia and daughter Una were originally buried in England. However, in June 2006, they were reinterred in plots adjacent to Hawthorne.

Writings

Hawthorne had a particularly close relationship with his publishers William Ticknor and James Thomas Fields. Hawthorne once told Fields, "I care more for your good opinion than for that of a host of critics." In fact, it was Fields who convinced Hawthorne to turn The Scarlet Letter into a novel rather than a short story. Ticknor handled many of Hawthorne's personal matters, including the purchase of cigars, overseeing financial accounts, and even purchasing clothes. Ticknor died with Hawthorne at his side in Philadelphia in 1864; according to a friend, Hawthorne was left "apparently dazed".

Literary style and themes

Hawthorne's works belong to romanticism or, more specifically, dark romanticism, cautionary tales that suggest that guilt, sin, and evil are the most inherent natural qualities of humanity. Many of his works are inspired by Puritan New England, combining historical romance loaded with symbolism and deep psychological themes, bordering on surrealism. His depictions of the past are a version of historical fiction used only as a vehicle to express common themes of ancestral sin, guilt and retribution. His later writings also reflect his negative view of the Transcendentalism movement.

Hawthorne was predominantly a short story writer in his early career. Upon publishing Twice-Told Tales, however, he noted, "I do not think much of them," and he expected little response from the public. His four major romances were written between 1850 and 1860: The Scarlet Letter (1850), The House of the Seven Gables (1851), The Blithedale Romance (1852) and The Marble Faun (1860). Another novel-length romance, Fanshawe, was published anonymously in 1828. Hawthorne defined a romance as being radically different from a novel by not being concerned with the possible or probable course of ordinary experience. In the preface to The House of the Seven Gables, Hawthorne describes his romance-writing as using "atmospherical medium as to bring out or mellow the lights and deepen and enrich the shadows of the picture". The picture, Daniel Hoffman found, was one of "the primitive energies of fecundity and creation."

Critics have applied feminist perspectives and historicist approaches to Hawthorne's depictions of women. Feminist scholars are interested particularly in Hester Prynne: they recognize that while she herself could not be the "destined prophetess" of the future, the "angel and apostle of the coming revelation" must nevertheless "be a woman." Camille Paglia saw Hester as mystical, "a wandering goddess still bearing the mark of her Asiatic origins ... moving serenely in the magic circle of her sexual nature". Lauren Berlant termed Hester "the citizen as woman [personifying] love as a quality of the body that contains the purest light of nature," her resulting "traitorous political theory" a "Female Symbolic" literalization of futile Puritan metaphors. Historicists view Hester as a protofeminist and avatar of the self-reliance and responsibility that led to women's suffrage and reproductive emancipation. Anthony Splendora found her literary genealogy among other archetypally fallen but redeemed women, both historic and mythic. As examples, he offers Psyche of ancient legend; Heloise of twelfth-century France's tragedy involving world-renowned philosopher Peter Abelard; Anne Hutchinson (America's first heretic, circa 1636), and Hawthorne family friend Margaret Fuller. In Hester's first appearance, Hawthorne likens her, "infant at her bosom", to Mary, Mother of Jesus, "the image of Divine Maternity". In her study of Victorian literature, in which such "galvanic outcasts" as Hester feature prominently, Nina Auerbach went so far as to name Hester's fall and subsequent redemption, "the novel's one unequivocally religious activity". Regarding Hester as a deity figure, Meredith A. Powers found in Hester's characterization "the earliest in American fiction that the archetypal Goddess appears quite graphically," like a Goddess "not the wife of traditional marriage, permanently subject to a male overlord"; Powers noted "her syncretism, her flexibility, her inherent ability to alter and so avoid the defeat of secondary status in a goal-oriented civilization".

Aside from Hester Prynne, the model women of Hawthorne's other novels—from Ellen Langton of Fanshawe to Zenobia and Priscilla of The Blithedale Romance, Hilda and Miriam of The Marble Faun and Phoebe and Hepzibah of The House of the Seven Gables—are more fully realized than his male characters, who merely orbit them. This observation is equally true of his short-stories, in which central females serve as allegorical figures: Rappaccini's beautiful but life-altering, garden-bound, daughter; almost-perfect Georgiana of "The Birthmark"; the sinned-against (abandoned) Ester of "Ethan Brand"; and goodwife Faith Brown, linchpin of Young Goodman Brown's very belief in God. "My Faith is gone!" Brown exclaims in despair upon seeing his wife at the Witches' Sabbath. Perhaps the most sweeping statement of Hawthorne's impetus comes from Mark Van Doren: "Somewhere, if not in the New England of his time, Hawthorne unearthed the image of a goddess supreme in beauty and power."

Hawthorne also wrote nonfiction. In 2008, the Library of America selected Hawthorne's "A show of wax-figures" for inclusion in its two-century retrospective of American True Crime.

Criticism

In "Hawthorne and His Mosses", Herman Melville wrote a passionate argument for Hawthorne to be among the burgeoning American literary canon, "He is one of the new, and far better generation of your writers." In this review of Mosses from an Old Manse, Melville describes an affinity for Hawthorne that would only increase: "I feel that this Hawthorne has dropped germinous seeds into my soul. He expands and deepens down, the more I contemplate him; and further, and further, shoots his strong New-England roots into the hot soil of my Southern soul." Edgar Allan Poe wrote important reviews of both Twice-Told Tales and Mosses from an Old Manse. Poe's assessment was partly informed by his contempt of allegory and moral tales, and his chronic accusations of plagiarism, though he admitted,

> The style of Mr. Hawthorne is purity itself. His tone is singularly effective—wild, plaintive, thoughtful, and in full accordance with his themes ... We look upon him as one of the few men of indisputable genius to whom our country has as yet given birth.

Ralph Waldo Emerson wrote, "Nathaniel Hawthorne's reputation as a writer is a very pleasing fact, because his writing is not good for anything, and this is a tribute to the man." Henry James praised Hawthorne, saying, "The fine thing in Hawthorne is that he cared for the deeper psychology, and that, in his way, he tried to become familiar with it." Poet John Greenleaf Whittier wrote that he admired the "weird and subtle beauty" in Hawthorne's tales. Evert Augustus Duyckinck said of Hawthorne, "Of the American writers destined to live, he is the most original, the one least indebted to foreign models or literary precedents of any kind."

Contemporary response to Hawthorne's work praised his sentimentality and moral purity while more modern evaluations focus on the dark psychological complexity. Beginning in the 1950s, critics have focused on symbolism and didacticism.

The critic Harold Bloom opined that only Henry James and William Faulkner challenge Hawthorne's position as the greatest American novelist, although he admitted that he favored James as the greatest American novelist.

Bloom saw Hawthorne's greatest works to be principally The Scarlet Letter, followed by The Marble Faun and certain short stories, including "My Kinsman, Major Molineux", "Young Goodman Brown", "Wakefield", and "Feathertop". (Source: Wikipedia)

NOTABLE WORKS

NOVELS

Fanshawe (published anonymously, 1828)

The Scarlet Letter (1850)

The House of the Seven Gables (1851)

The Blithedale Romance (1852)

The Marble Faun: Or, The Romance of Monte Beni (1860) (as Transformation: Or, The Romance of Monte Beni, UK publication, same year)

The Dolliver Romance (1863) (unfinished)

Septimius Felton; or, the Elixir of Life (unfinished, published in the Atlantic Monthly, 1872)

Doctor Grimshawe's Secret: A Romance (unfinished, with preface and notes by Julian Hawthorne, 1882)

SHORT STORY COLLECTIONS

Twice-Told Tales (1837)

Grandfather's Chair (1840)

Mosses from an Old Manse (1846)

A Wonder-Book for Girls and Boys (1851)

The Snow-Image, and Other Twice-Told Tales (1852)

Tanglewood Tales (1853)

The Dolliver Romance and Other Pieces (1876)

The Great Stone Face and Other Tales of the White Mountains (1889)

SELECTED SHORT STORIES

"The Hollow of the Three Hills" (1830)

"Roger Malvin's Burial" (1832)

"My Kinsman, Major Molineux" (1832)

"The Minister's Black Veil" (1832)

"Young Goodman Brown" (1835)

"The Gray Champion" (1835)

"The White Old Maid" (1835)

"Wakefield" (1835)

"The Ambitious Guest" (1835)

"The Man of Adamant" (1837)

"The May-Pole of Merry Mount" (1837)

"The Great Carbuncle" (1837)

"Dr. Heidegger's Experiment" (1837)

"A Virtuoso's Collection" (May 1842)

"The Birth-Mark" (March 1843)

"The Celestial Railroad" (1843)

"Egotism; or, The Bosom-Serpent" (1843)

"Earth's Holocaust" (1844)

"Rappaccini's Daughter" (1844)

"P.'s Correspondence" (1845)

"The Artist of the Beautiful" (1846)

"Fire Worship" (1846)

"Ethan Brand" (1850)

"The Great Stone Face" (1850)

"Feathertop" (1852)

NONFICTION

Twenty Days with Julian & Little Bunny (written 1851, published 1904)

Our Old Home (1863)

Passages from the French and Italian Notebooks (1871)

CPSIA information can be obtained
at www.ICGtesting.com
Printed in the USA
LVHW091701170720
660560LV00051B/418